SLEEPY Time OLie

by
William
Joyce

LAURA GERINGER BOOKS
An Imprint of HarperCollins Publishers

It's Rolie Polie evening.
The Rolie day is ending.
Sleepy eyes are everywhere—
the moon,
the house,
the rocking chair,
and Olie's Rolie Polie bear.

Rolie Polie evening—
Olie's almost sleeping.
His Rolie days are without care,
especially when Pappy's there
reading in his rocking chair.

It's late enough.
He should be there.
But where is Pappy?
Where oh,
oh where?

Rolie Polie

evening—

What is all that

squeaking?

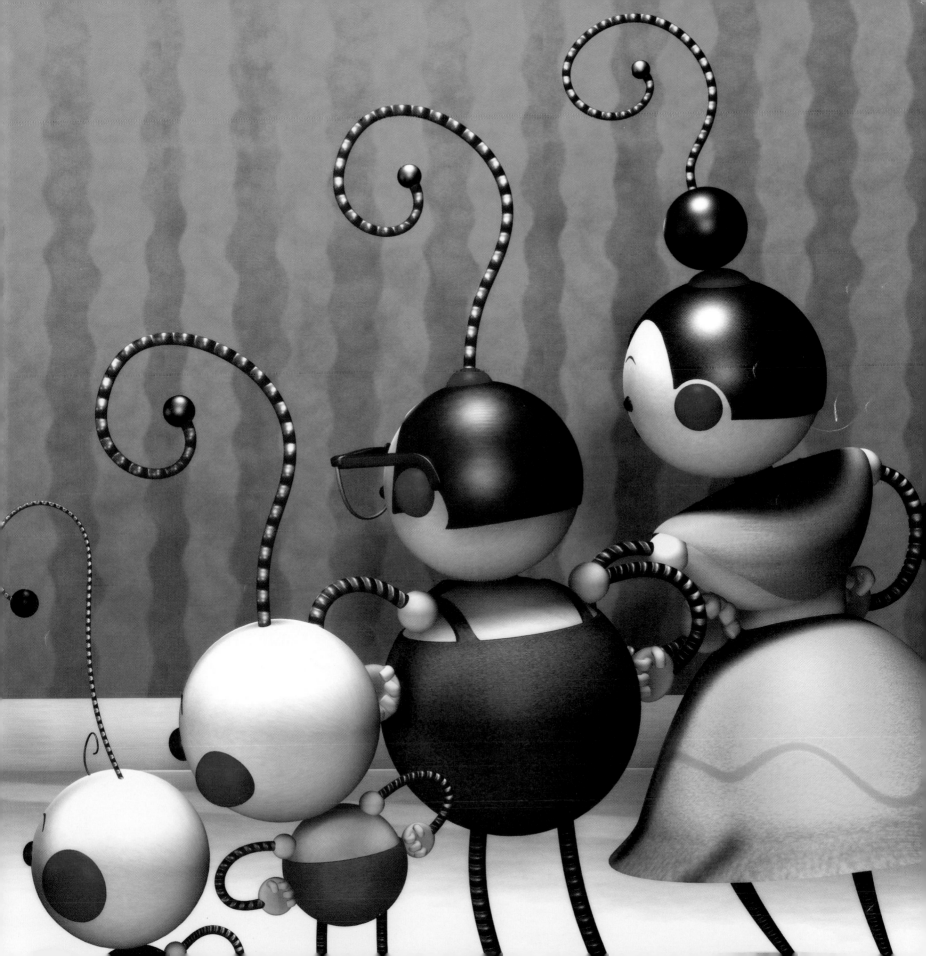

Pappy comes in
all unwound.
"I bonked my head.
I just fell down.
I broke my smile.
I can't unfrown.
I might as well
get out of town . . .

". . . .my heart has lost its swing,
my legs have lost their sway.
My step has not a bit of spring,
my hip has no hooray.
I feel old and all kerploppy—
I'm a walking junk parade.
My cheeks do not feel cheeky.
My red-letter day has grayed."

So he rolied into bed
and that's exactly where he stayed.

But Olie knew just what to do
to make old Pappy feel like new.
"I'll make a super silly ray!"
excitedly said Olie.
"And with it I will save the day
for all things Rolie Polie!"

He grabbed
a goofy this
and a very doofy that,
a hammer
nicknamed Phyllis
and a most peculiar hat.
An extremely funny bone
shaped rather
like a pelvis, and a shot
of Uncle Gizmo
as he danced around
like Elvis . . .

. . . a single Zowie
hopscotch hop,
a book of jokes that
laughed nonstop,
a really, really
loud hiccup
supplied by Spot—
he's some swell pup!

Then Olie burst
into the room
and with his ray
dispelled the gloom.
"I made a Pappy
pick-me-up
to help old Pappy
ungrow-up."

Then Pappy grinned as, deep inside,

his silly gear began to glide.

It tickled every Pappy part,

it ungrew-up his sad old heart.

Up and out young Pappy flew,

feeling happy and brand-new.

They walked on walls,
swirled through the air,
and danced around
in bubbles.
If robots spend
the day that way,
they can't have any
troubles.

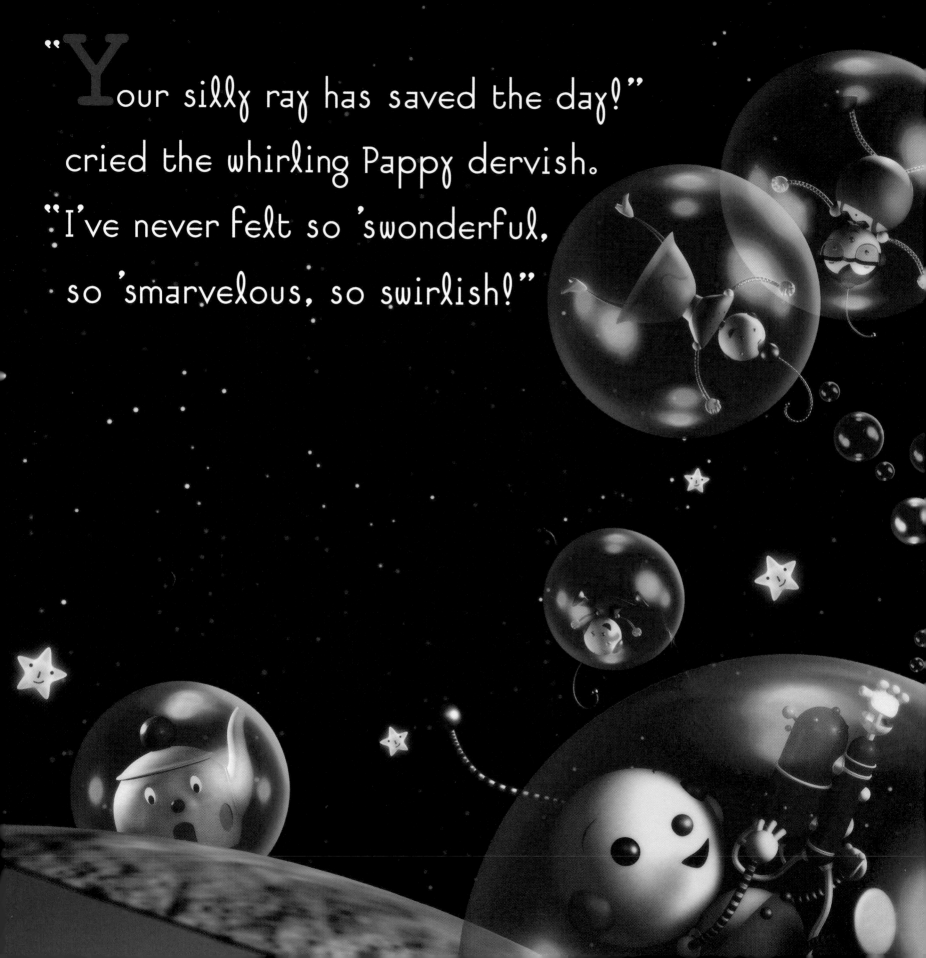

"Your silly ray has saved the day!"
cried the whirling Pappy dervish.
"I've never felt so 'swonderful,
so 'smarvelous, so swirlish!"

The Rolie moon and stars and sun
joined in the happy Pappy fun.
And when the Polie fun was done,
they bubbled homeward one by one.

Rolie Polie evening—
the house will soon be sleeping.

Jammies on for all robots.

They're moving slow, they're yawning lots,
they're wearing Rolie polka dots.

Rolie Polie evening—
Olie's day is ending.
Happy Pappy, warm and wise,
reads lullabies and hushabies
beneath the sleepy Rolie skies.

Rolie Polie evening—
Olie now is sleeping.
His dreams are filled
with silly rays
and hip hoorays
and happy
Pappy holidays.
All Rolie dreams
are without care
especially if
Pappy's there.

Rolie Polie evening—
everything is sleeping—
the moon,
the house,
the rocking chair....

Everything . . .

everywhere . . .

is sleeping now
without a care.

The end

z z Z z